ISBN 979-8-9897701-3-7

Published by Hidden Hand Press
www.hiddenhandbooks.com

VALTOHA

by
Hamant Singh

ACKNOWLEDGEMENTS

There is a long list of people to thank and it is my deepest hope that no deserving people have been overlooked in this section. My brain is a constantly disorganised mess that flits from thought to thought very quickly. I've deliberately put a lot of effort into this section so that I do not miss anyone that has contributed to this text.

Firstly, I would like to thank my parents, Manjit Singh and Nimmi John. Thank you for being such a huge part of the adventure to Punjab, for digging up all the forgotten information and for everything else that you've done to see this book published. Had it not been for your tireless detective work, I would've had very little to write about. I love you both and want you to know that you're both a very big part of this book. My brother, Reuben Singh, the crown Prince of Valtoha! We will always have a claim, I don't care what anyone says! Thank you for helping to organise so many little crucial things along the way. You're a big part of the book and none of this would've been possible without your help.

An extension of these integral thanks goes out to Gabriela, mi amor. Thank you for braving the tides and travelling with us to the most remote areas of Punjab. Your open-mindedness and love have contributed so much to my work. Thank you for setting me on this course and encouraging me to publish as well. You and my parents have made our Indian journey so much more fun and I won't soon forget all our memories. You are about to become my wife and I could ask for no one better in my life. I love you.

A special mention goes out to my extended family all over the world. To all those in Singapore, Punjab, Malaysia, Kerala, Australia, England, Canada and Mexico. Even though I may be the linking common denominator, I'm proud of how diverse and far we have travelled.

To Shane Reilly for going through hours and hours of beer, whiskey and intense deliberation. I don't have many friends and find myself fortunate to count you among the few. Thank you for being instigators, voices of reason and nurturers toward my various endeavours. Also, thanks for the picture edits you've helped with in this book, Shane.

Another dear friend who deserves his own section here is Dr. Ho Jiaxuan, the editor of the last book, this one, and is forever cursed to edit my work. Thank you for your guidance, discourse and some of the most enjoyable moments of my life. No one has contributed directly more to my writing than you. My most treasured friend, my confidant and my (second) biggest critic.

May we take some secrets to our graves but hide others in books, art and music for people to find.

To my friends, writers and trusted advisors: Jeremy Fernando, Pedro Tsamaxan and Katherine Schneider. Thank you for the advice, honest critique and help in my journey to where I am today. Special thanks goes out to my aunt, Gurdip Kaur, the National Library Board (Singapore) and The National Archives (Singapore). This book was difficult enough to write and not having the resources made it even trickier. Each of you or your establishments has helped in one way or another to acquire more information and resources about my grandfather and made this book possible. Also, I would like to express my gratitude to Dr. (Prof.) Kirpal Singh for his involvement and the foreword to this book.

Special thanks to all the other establishments in Mexico and the US who've supported my book tour of May 2023. It's been an experience and I've met so many that I imagine to be lifelong companions on my artistic journey.

FOREWORD
BY
DR. KIRPAL SINGH

Ever since Alex Haley gave us *Roots*, we have become accustomed to reading stories and books detailing the history of individuals and communities and nations. Searching for one's *Roots* is nowadays taken for granted as are the often astounding details revealed by many who embark on tracing their roots. Our author Hamant has done a wonderful job of exploring his family roots and trying to cement his findings with received wisdom as well as current notions associated with the somewhat nebulous notions of continuity and change. Hamant writes astutely and his grasp of detail is quite extraordinary – giving us both confidence as well as provoking us to reflect and consider our own inheritances and legacies.

Hamant's exploratory journey should provide inspiration to all who are on a voyage of discovery vis-a-vis roots. It has to be remembered that not all such journeys are comforting – many are like the journey described by Hamant – bewildering at times and even puzzling. However, once travelled honestly and bravely, the sense of security and even the notion of " homecoming" is something to be proud of.

- Dr. (Prof.) Kirpal Singh

PREFACE

The story that follows chronicles a search for my past. It started with a wild hunt for more details about my grandfather, who passed away tragically when my father was only 12. This is why there's very little known about him in general. The quest for details intensified and culminated in our decision to go to India and to quite literally, seek his village out. I eventually went there with my parents and girlfriend but it wasn't a simple decision.

The following true story is an account of the search for my grandfather. Names have not been changed to protect identities. Rather, they have been kept the same to draw attention to the lives and individuals mentioned. It is a story with quite a few different characters involved. The function of each character will reveal itself, as their uniqueness will determine their roles in the story.

This story is certainly not one borne out of sheer luck. I conducted as much research as possible before, during and after the trip. While one could say that there was some luck involved in my grandfather's voyage to Singapore, his struggle to reach Singapore must have been just as hard as ours to reach Valtoha. I suppose the struggle was on both ends to reach this stage but neither of us knew it at the time. Attributing events to 'luck' has a way of cheapening or humbling the effort and energy that goes into an endeavour. This is why I prefer to refrain from using that word when talking about the way things have come together in the way that they have. I think that it also gives meaning and empowers the effort and actions of the people involved.

While the content is absolutely factual, the form of the text was inspired by the 2016 film, *Ardaas*. In this film, one of the characters is a little girl who writes letters to God that go unanswered. I wrote to my grandfather but kept letters hidden like it was something embarrassing or ridiculous. Perhaps it was just meant to be private because right now, I'm certainly not embarrassed. On the contrary, I'm actually very proud; or should I say, I've *grown* to be very proud of this 'communication'. It didn't start out this way but it's turned into a real record of development, thought and wonder. Unanswered letters, is in itself, a complicated concept. We usually seek replies or responses to our letters, much like the little girl in *Ardaas*. Unlike her, I did not expect a reply and turned my letters to my grandfather into therapy, a diary and a confessional all at once. Oftentimes, the lack of a response to the sound of your own voice naturally results in deep reflection and ironically, answers. This is not a story of one man but a plural one. It may have begun with me searching for my grandfather, two people who have never met but yearn to, at least once. Alas, there is no way we could've met since he is no longer alive. However, the search quickly turned into one family searching for another. One family searching and *finding* another; another that had always been alive. The family is now split; some have remained in India, some are in Singapore, others in Australia, Malaysia, even as far as the US and the UK. I myself live in Mexico. In many ways, the events of this book have motivated conversations between these family members. Many have lost touch despite being from the same generation. It is easy to forget our past when we're preoccupied with our present. Some want to forget their past but it is clear that this is not the case with the characters in this story.

There's no denying that this story is very personal and perhaps may not resonate with some readers. However, we've all lost someone at some point and wished that we knew them better. Specifically speaking, I'm sure I'm not alone in not knowing my grandparents. I can only imagine the number of immigrants and locals that have never met their grandparents in Singapore. There's a good chance that this is also a commonplace occurrence in Canada, Australia, the UK and other countries with significant immigration, historically or in the present moment. It's quite clear that something that I imagined to be personal isn't quite as unique as I initially made it out to be in my head. To those who read this book and are able to relate to it, I hope this inspires you to go on your own search for your family history; to dig up your own roots, so to speak. It quite possibly may be completely irrelevant to the lives you're living right now but you never know what you may find if you don't go looking for it.

Finally, this story is a tribute to the people of Punjab, Amarkot, Valtoha and all other Punjabis around the world. The resilience that you've shown against threats from within and without makes you worthy of the honour and respect given to your last names. The Jallianwala Bagh Massacre and 1984 Anti-Sikh riots are only two of the most notable examples that illustrate the strength of the Sikh race. To all the people mentioned in this story, your smiles and warmth will not be soon forgotten. To my newfound family, to whom I feel simultaneously attached and completely detached from, this is dedicated to you. I intend to make your stories known to the world, or should I say, *our* stories. The very nature of these stories may be a difficult read in its entirety but there's a story for everyone. This is mine and I love my story. I hope you enjoy reading it as much as I have writing it.

Waheguruji ka Khalsa, Waheguruji ki Fateh.

You. Elusive man. Ghost man. My grandfather.

I didn't know much about you growing up; just your name, Singara Singh Valtoha[1]. Sometimes spelt Singhara, sometimes Shingara. A lot is lost in translation, I suppose. A lot is lost in memory too, for that matter. There's a dusty, black and white picture of you in the altar room, next to your wife's. Incense, bananas and all that, as if these things would keep your memory alive. At least I got to know my *Dadiji*[2] for a few years before she passed. I was young but I am not anymore. And somehow, you still remain a ghost to me. I'm all grown up but I still don't know much about you. The years haven't changed much of our relationship. I've decided to write my thoughts to you but I don't know why, though? It's not as if you're around to read them or comment on them, never mind reply.

You are a ghost in the truest sense. Dead, lurking and haunting. Your shadow has always hung over my father and even over me in some ways. I can't even properly

---

[1] In India during British rule, it was not uncommon for one's last name to be either their caste or in this case, your town's name.

[2] A respectful term for one's paternal grandmother.

call it your memory because remembering takes knowing you in the first place.

This is the tricky bit: I am of your bloodline but it doesn't mean anything if I don't know my heritage. I've always felt so far removed from Punjabi culture and Sikhism, in general. Not like any of this is your fault; it just is. Moving away from India automatically means distance, but forgetting is another thing altogether. The other Sikh boys I know at school are mostly the same; turbanless, beardless and clueless. Urban Turbans I think is what the more traditional Sikhs call us. So, how Sikh am I then? Even the name-bearing, blood-carrying half of me can't quite claim anything. Neither you nor I can fix this situation, though? At least, I don't have any ideas and you? You're very dead.

The story I've heard goes something along the lines that at some point, you had decided to come to Singapore and leave it all behind. I wonder why, though? Were you in search of a better life? You certainly didn't find one here because life was tough. In some ways, staying back there would've been the easier, more convenient choice. You gave up familiarity, friends and family in the hopes of a more promising future. You learnt new languages and ways of a mixed culture. I wonder if it was just desire or the consequence of a better life, the Promised Land, perhaps for yourself or perhaps for the future generations. Another part of me considers if you had been running from something in India, though.

I often wonder what would've been if you had not left. Would I have been the son of a farmer, who was the son of a farmer? It probably would've been too much effort to break the cycle. It would've been too comfortable to begin yearning for something different. Not better, since the farm life isn't bad at all. Would I have risked it all to head to the capital to make something else of myself? I can't tell since there's no real way of knowing what would've gone differently if we'd changed one little detail. There's no use in wondering either since the present is all that is real and truly matters. To wonder about these things is to fantasise about pointless fantasies. We're all products of the circumstances where we're born, I suppose.

Your passing was somewhat premature, though. You had departed before being able to see your labour come into fruition. Labour, literal labour was what you came here for. They say that you worked as a driver, a lorry I think? I guess you could never sit still, could you? Always on the move, Valtoha to Singapore, point A to point B. Now death has finally trapped you in one spot. You sit there watching it all unfold from a dusty, black and white picture in the corner of the altar room. I know you're in the corner somewhere, lurking, looking at us now 60 years later. You're probably watching me write this letter to you, screaming your replies that fall on my deaf ears.

Did you haunt the guy who killed you? Do you haunt him still? He'd somehow managed to cut your life short but didn't end all your dreams. You did, in fact, make a better life for your descendants. We wouldn't be where we were had you not come this way. There's a mixture of shame and irony, that we can't say we remember you every day. Again, remembering is hard since it requires knowing first. We commemorate though, once a year. We light a fire and pay our due respects for your sacrifice, your risk, your life and your death. Clearly, not enough. I hope at least the haunting of him would've made up for it. You don't seem like the vengeful sort but I have known your memory to be particularly haunting.

I'm a huge fan of horror and maybe it's because I've always had your ghost hanging around me. It appears you've inspired me even in death – through death and unknowing. I've always theorised that all fears stem from a fear of the unknown. The fear of the dark, for instance, is a fear that stems from not being able to see and therefore, creates the discomfort of not knowing. The same goes with the fear of heights, spiders and all the others. They all come from a place of not truly knowing because if one did, it would no longer be fear as much as trauma.

I think I have more questions than answers because of how elusive you were. Perhaps there is an actual genuine fear of knowing. What might I find if I walked into Valtoha? Answers to my questions? Most definitely! More secrets, I imagine. Your very nature guarantees it! Unrequited love? Enemies? Were you a criminal on the run from the law? The unknown begins by making the mind wander, then run and finally gradually descend into an abyss of insanity. My mind just makes me wonder if you were a ghost even during your lifetime. The kind of man that would walk into a bar and occupy the seat in the corner, unnoticed. The kind of man that would deliberately make the effort to disappear into a crowded street. The kind of man that would find it so difficult to stand out. That kind of man, a lot like me; my kind of man.

I still don't know much about you, just your name – Singara Singh Valtoha. *Mere dadaji*[3]. Whoever you were…

---

[3] Translates directly to "my grandfather" in Punjabi.

You would've been proud, I think? Proud of your son, my father. It must've been hard for him to have a complete, developed idea of what fatherhood is. You passed when puberty was just dawning on him. With no brothers, he was forced to shape his own idea of what a man needed to be. Surely, his memories of you must have played a part in shaping some of his approach to it. Still, he was only a boy then. With no uncles or older brothers, he was left with his adopted younger brother, Segar, to figure out what it meant to be a man and then, a father. I don't suppose I'm allowed to comment too much since I'm not a father, still just a son. Despite this, I think he's managed to become the best father any son could ask for.

When my father speaks of you, he remembers you as a pillar of responsibility. He remembers how you'd always be there with the warm smell of a baguette and Churn butter from the nearby bakery in the mornings. How the whole family would all have breakfast together before hurrying off to school or work. You made it so that your wife and children all began and ended their days as a family. He particularly remembers your Sundays together that began in the gurdwara [4] at Wilkie Road. The breakfasts there that came with morning prayers

---

[4] A Sikh temple.

and then watching the news on TV at the nearby Community Centre as the afternoon dwindled away. He remembers your devotion to God and how you abstained from alcohol and tobacco, probably realising the unnecessity of it all. He remembers.

My father says that you were a man of very few words, slow to anger and very loving in general. You saw to the needs of all your children; made sure they had all they needed and a bit more. All your children seem to remember you in the exact same way which is unusual. Multiple perspectives have a way of spinning diverse narratives but this doesn't seem to be the case here. I imagine that you must've been fair to all of them and this is why they all hold you similarly in their memories. That strong responsible father who made his children happy. That pillar of a man that kept the proverbial roof up.

Your son had worked two jobs to see me born since just the one wasn't providing enough. By day, he was a government servant, working his way up the ranks; watched by the public eye and expected to be that model citizen. By night, a watchman. A servant to a business but hidden away like a ghost. Barely seen by anyone in the company and almost turning into a myth of some kind. No one in that building knew who guarded the place at night, nor did they need to. He wandered and functioned as an unseen guardian. Extra income aside, he may have ironically, learnt aspects of fatherhood as well in this way. You may have instilled the basics of manhood in him but maybe life was the one who taught fatherhood. What is a father beyond fathering a child? A model citizen, a protective spirit? Somewhere in between? Where does it begin and end? Does it begin when your wife announces pregnancy or before that? I'm tempted to say that fatherhood ends at the end of one's child's life. Perhaps it is a concept that lives on much longer than what I imagine. A part of me thinks that I'm starting to understand ancestral worship. Perhaps one day I will know; when son becomes father.

You fulfilled those roles when you were alive and you're fondly remembered for it. We all still invoke the name over a game of cards. "VALTOHA!" is what we yell when we get a good hand. It gives us away but there's something essential in yelling it out loud. Valtoha has become a bit of a promised land to my brother and I, I think? It's our victory cry much like Vikings cry out, "To Valhalla!" It unveils a lot about our desires to visit the 'motherland'. That same land you left all those years ago. My brother and I speak a lot about it, about what it would be like to visit. My brother and I are grandsons you would've been very proud of, as little as we know. We're lions, the both of us. Proper little Singhs.

My brother and I haven't had the best relationship when we were younger but I've seen it blossom into respect.

We used to fight a lot, as young lions do. However, with two strong beasts of boys, there comes an inevitable point where we can't help but acknowledge what we've individually built and achieved over the years. You would've been proud of us, if only you were here to see.

Perhaps the urge to rediscover our past wouldn't have been as strong as if you were here. You'd tell us stories and we'd know you better, which is really what we would've wanted. It wouldn't have made us wonder though now, would it? In many ways, the myth and legend of Valtoha exists because you don't. I really hope we get to see it one day as brothers, to discover Valtoha as grandsons in search of our grandfather's village.

Today I went to war with your son. I don't think we've ever exchanged words the way we did today; we exchanged anger is what actually happened.

I've finished a four-year course in English and can't wait to hit the job market. My graduation is coming up and I want to begin working as soon as I can. No opportunities have come my way except a job offer in Mandalay, Myanmar. I've quite literally applied for over a hundred jobs and the only one that responded was a teaching position that would see me based there. Full disclosure, it's been one of the jobs I'd been avoiding my whole life. I used to laugh at my teachers that they had to prepare work, grade it and then go through the mistakes with their students. All I had to do was take the work and write some rubbish in it, completely unaccountable. It was their job to worry about what nonsense I'd scribbled and submitted. I may not have had an idea of what I wanted to be, but I thought I was quite certain that I knew what I didn't want! Alas, I now find myself in this situation and it is life that is laughing at me.

Of course, my father was absolutely livid when I told him that I'd made up my mind to leave. There were literally no opportunities for me in Singapore despite being a fresh graduate. You'd think that would've meant something; I know I did! Yet, here I am faced with the assurance of guaranteed employment, but outside where I had grown up. I'd love to stay if that meant I could work here, but there seems to be nothing for me here. You would've stayed in Valtoha if there were opportunities, I imagine. Or were you running? I don't have anything to run from at the moment. Either way, one thing's for certain. In your own position, you saw it fit to leave just as I do now.

I see my father's wrath and I understand his arguments. Unfortunately, I'm not quite sure he sees mine. He's paid a ton of money to send me through university and here I am using my degree to move to a militarised, third world country to teach. It's obvious that every father wants the best for his son and surely my father is no different. Perhaps, it's fear that's fuelling his anger, the fear of unknown areas with less comforts than our own. He's known hardship and has worked himself to the bone to give us a comfortable life. He must think me mad for wanting to return to a more difficult one! He must think me mad for wanting to leave the life that you planted the seed for. You came here with a better life in mind and here we are doing well enough. Behold! This fool of a grandson, this madman who wants to go teach in the countryside of Myanmar. That degree may have meant that I completed the course, but clearly doesn't reflect the fact that I'm not very bright.

My mother calmly tried to get between the two of us and make us see reason. She quite literally was the eye of the hurricane. The hardest part is that I know my father means well. This is probably a situation where we both think we're right. Should it surprise him, really? I must get it from somewhere, mustn't I? Son of my father – your son. It's all quite surprising since you were described to me as a calm, level-headed man. I wonder if anyone tried to stop you leaving Valtoha or if you just didn't have that many friends that tried to hold you back. My guess is some of your friends left Valtoha with you, too. I suppose one can only be as stubborn as those who try to hold you back, whatever that endeavour may be.

I think he's cooled down now, I know I have. I'm going to apologise to him and explain that I'm only doing this for myself. Call me traditional but I want his blessing; he is my father after all. Also, I want to put an end to this drama; he's my father and I want him to be on my side. It hurts and it's so painful that I'm in tears. It hurts me that it feels like I hurt him because it certainly wasn't my intention. Perhaps it takes some people a bit longer to see things. There are many things that blind someone: ego, anger, experience, perceptions, the list goes on. It doesn't change who he is, who I am or who he is to me.

I'm off to speak to him now. I realise now how cathartic

speaking to the dead is. Thank you for being there, even though you aren't. You've strangely managed to teach me something from beyond the grave by making me reflect on how you lived your life.

Growing up without you was particularly hard. I'm older now so I'm quite over it but there still is a nagging desire to know who you were. It's not the same way one desires to see an old ex-girlfriend again or the desire to make up with an old friend over a squabble. It's the kind of stressful need to find the missing pieces in a puzzle. I know what the general picture looks like but the missing pieces are from smaller framed settings within the big picture. What would it change, though? I've spent all my life without you around so what's the need to fill up the missing pieces in the puzzle? A lorry still runs without some parts, sometimes; as long as they aren't essential parts. How essential is my past, then? I have been running through life with parts missing. Not parts essential to living life and progressing, but parts I really want to include in my machinery.

What use is a carpet or piece of tapestry with holes in it? Not entirely useless, but the incompleteness is certainly an issue, both aesthetically and functionally. And there is no other reason for this, other than that it simply must be there. My life is more of a quilt than tapestry with a unified design. The things I've done and the things I've experienced traverse different continents, cultures and lifestyles. Perhaps all these exotic patches have been the result of the subconscious search for more integral ones. A compensation, if you would? As if the diversity would make up for gaps, for inadequacies.

Not that there's anything wrong with more unified designs of tapestry or puzzle designs that have sections flowing into each other. In many ways, these unified designs are more cohesive and pleasing to the eye; some might even say more beautiful. My life isn't quite the same but who are we meant to please anyway? I don't think anyone's tapestry of life is ever quite beautiful. Is it enough for me? Yes, it has been for the longest time. Let's say, the 'quilt' has functioned satisfactorily. I still would have liked the option to have your stories woven into mine. As I imagine you would've wanted our patches woven into yours – a more wholesome tapestry of stories, people and experiences. To know what struggles and joy I've seen; to see your children develop into the mature adults that they are and then have a new generation of their own. I yearn for the more wholesome tapestry to keep me warm.

I'm in a particularly philosophical mood tonight, I suppose. Then again, nights are the best parts of the day for self-reflection. You must've done the same at

night, lying on a *manjaa* [5] under a sea of stars.
Surrounded by silence all around you, save for the
ornamental chirps of nearby insects. In the arms of my
imagination, it all seems very pulchritudinous. That is
the perfect word since I could never truly know the
beauty of those old, simple nights filled with stars,
silence and dreams. Staring at that open infinity that
made you think. The thoughts then probably wandered
into wonder. What if I left this place? Where would I go?
Would I ever want to come back? The reflections then
must've sailed you to the conclusion that you had to
leave at some point. Valtoha was not for you just as you
were not made for it.

In the dead of my nights, I reflect. I reflect on the values
that I was raised on. Those very same principles which
undeniably reflect the values you were raised on. And
the cycle goes on and on, even though it never quite is
that simple. You would've probably approved of me
moving away and discovering new things; collecting
new patches and sewing them directly into the quilt.

---

[5] A small bed made from a woven fabric stretched over a bamboo frame.

I'm writing this letter on a very long flight from Mexico to Singapore. My girlfriend is coming to visit and meet my parents. These days we have the luxury to travel long distances quite easily. I can't begin to imagine what travelling significant distances must've been like in the day.

The popular opinion is that you came on a ship, the SS Rajula in the 1940s. The journey must've taken about a week and some. I don't know which port you left from, but Ludhiana was the closest seaport in Punjab. I imagine you boarding the SS Rajula with whatever little money and possessions you had, quite literally embarking on a new journey in life. It was definitely the most affordable way to travel at the time and this was the ship that brought most Indians to Singapore during that period.

When we get to Singapore, we're going to begin a wee plan to visit India and hopefully find traces of you. There's been a breakthrough! My father has somehow got his hands on a digital copy of a letter from you to your brother, Bachan Singh. One of my aunts had found it, digitalised it and made it immortal. Bless her. It's addressed to Amarkot Post Office, though. While it isn't actually Valtoha, I think that may have been the only post office available at the time. I'm willing to bet there wasn't a post office in Valtoha at the time and I'm willing to bet there still isn't. We'll hopefully eventually get clues, get to Valtoha and ask around the village. Hopefully, we'll meet some of your old friends or see the fields you used to till. What started out as a frequently passed joke seems to be actually happening. We're planning it six months ahead and booking it way in advance. I just want to know more about you, really. I'd be grateful for any information, any new stories. You left Valtoha, wanting never to return and looking to start anew. It begins to feel like disappearing was something you were almost good at. Still, here we find ourselves longing to return to look for traces of you. The irony in our lives never ceases to amaze me. We're planning all this, knowing full well that we might find nothing. We're not expecting much, but it would be good for us to at least make the journey. To Valhalla! In all honesty, I don't think there's much left there to find, though. Your friends are probably all dead and I don't think there is any family left since Bachan Singh died.

Let me introduce you to her since she's about to meet the rest of the family. Her name is Gabriela and she's Mexican. A few years back, there was a big fuss made about a flu that had been going around at the time. I didn't want to remain in Singapore so I moved to México. It was the only country open at the time so I got vaccinated and moved there. I arrived, settled and met her a few days after moving there. I would love for you to have been able to actually meet her in person. Yes, not Punjabi, not even Indian, but there isn't a bad bone in her body. Imagine how it would have been to meet your daughter-in-law for the first time? If you'd let your only son marry a Malayalee, then this should be no big deal right? Times certainly have changed and surely you can understand that. Moving away from a small village in Punjab and then having a marriage that was not arranged was a real firebrand move. Well, at least I imagine it must've been. Still, good people are good people, I suppose? I'm sure you've known a few good ones and a few bad apples in your time.

You seem to have married really well though. My grandmother managed to raise the whole family on her own after you unexpectedly passed. How a mourning widow managed to raise five children, and then even adopt one more, is beyond me. After you passed, she found employment at a plant nursery in Braddell Road, raising even more little ones. Clearly you saw a heart of gold in a woman who was tough as nails. Women these days go on and on about being strong, tough and independent and they don't do very much, really. Gone are the days where women did what my *Dadiji* and my maternal grandmother did and didn't have the need to proclaim it to the world. Their struggles were daily and their struggles were real. They also didn't have all these media platforms to rant and rave about it all, like we do today. It was less words and more action on a daily basis. Come to think of it, even if these avenues of expression were available to them, they probably wouldn't have had the time to brag and gloat about overcoming their struggles.

I don't know much about women but I think really strong, independent women don't need validation from internet posts and t-shirt proclamations. In fact, their need for claps and cheers from other people quite literally shows dependence. If they were truly that tough, I think they'd already know. Either way, I don't think a dependent woman is 'weak' just like I don't think a dependent man is as well.

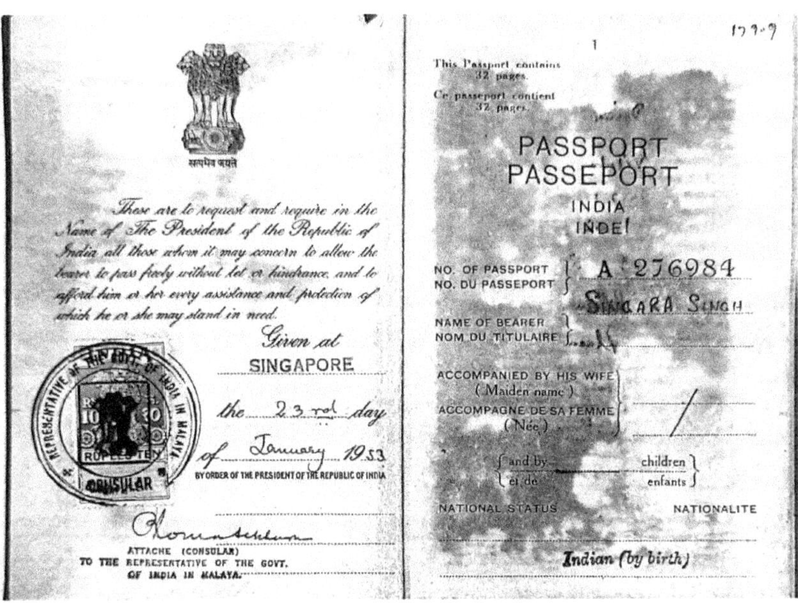

These are to request and require in the
Name of The President of the Republic of
India all those whom it may concern to allow the
bearer to pass freely without let or hindrance, and to
afford him or her every assistance and protection of
which he or she may stand in need.
Given at
SINGAPORE
the 23 rd day
of January 19 53
BY ORDER OF THE PRESIDENT OF THE REPUBLIC OF INDIA
ATTACHE (CONSULAR)
TO THE REPRESENTATIVE OF THE GOVT.
OF INDIA IN MALAYA.
This Passport contains
32 pages.
Ce passeport contient
32 pages.
PASSPORT
PASSEPORT
INDIA
INDE
NO. OF PASSPORT
NO. DU PASSEPORT
A 276984
NAME OF BEARER
NOM DU TITULAIRE
SINGARA SINGH
ACCOMPANIED BY HIS WIFE
(Maiden name)
ACCOMPAGNE DE SA FEMME
(Née)
and by
et de
children
enfants
NATIONAL STATUS
NATIONALITE
Indian (by birth)

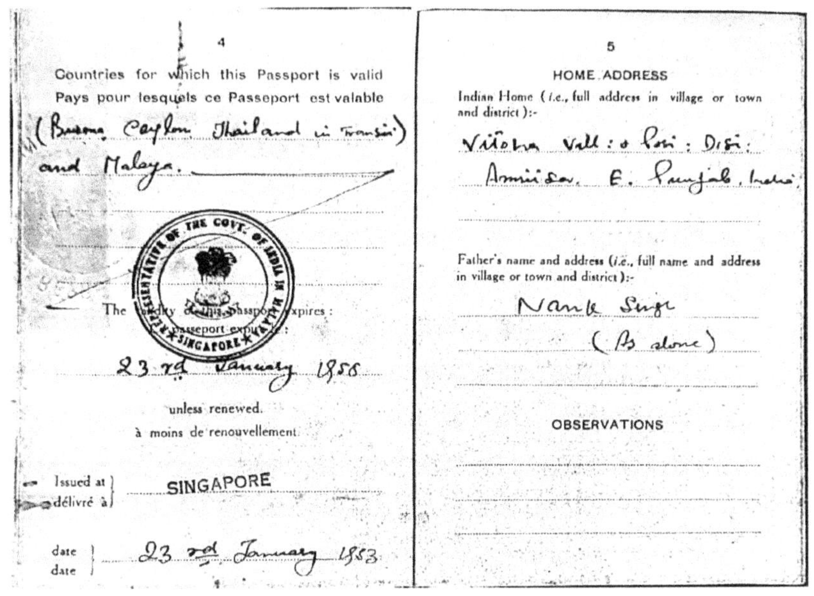

4
Countries for which this Passport is valid
Pays pour lesquels ce Passeport est valable
(Burma, Ceylon, Thailand in Transit)
and Malaya.
The validity of this Passport expires :
passeport expire :
23 rd January 1955
unless renewed.
à moins de renouvellement.
Issued at
délivré à
SINGAPORE
date
date
23 rd January 1953
5
HOME ADDRESS
Indian Home (i.e., full address in village or town
and district):-
Vitoha Vill : o Posi : Disi :
Amriisar. E. Punjab, India
Father's name and address (i.e., full name and address
in village or town and district):-
Nanak Singh
(As above)
OBSERVATIONS

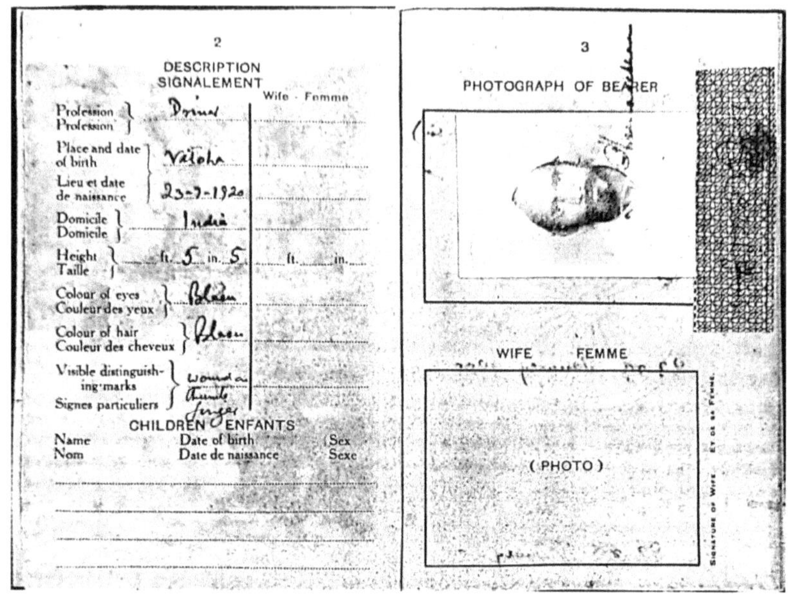

First few pages of my grandfather's passport, complete with handwritten mistakes.

I can think of a thousand different conversations I would've loved to have had with you. I have some of these conversations with my father, who's doubled up as a grandfather for me I suppose in some ways. He's a very wise, experienced man who I think would've loved these conversations with you too. He has perspectives to offer on marriage and women for sure, but I would've loved to hear yours too. I see how things differ over space and time and no doubt, you'd have some insight worth listening to. A lot of it may not be relevant but I

22

suppose some things don't really change with courting, with women and with love. I think we're all not that different, the three of us. Despite growing up in different eras and different economic conditions, there seem to have been some core values that survived. You spoke to your son at an early age and he spoke to his son. That same song did carry on the same wind through the ages.

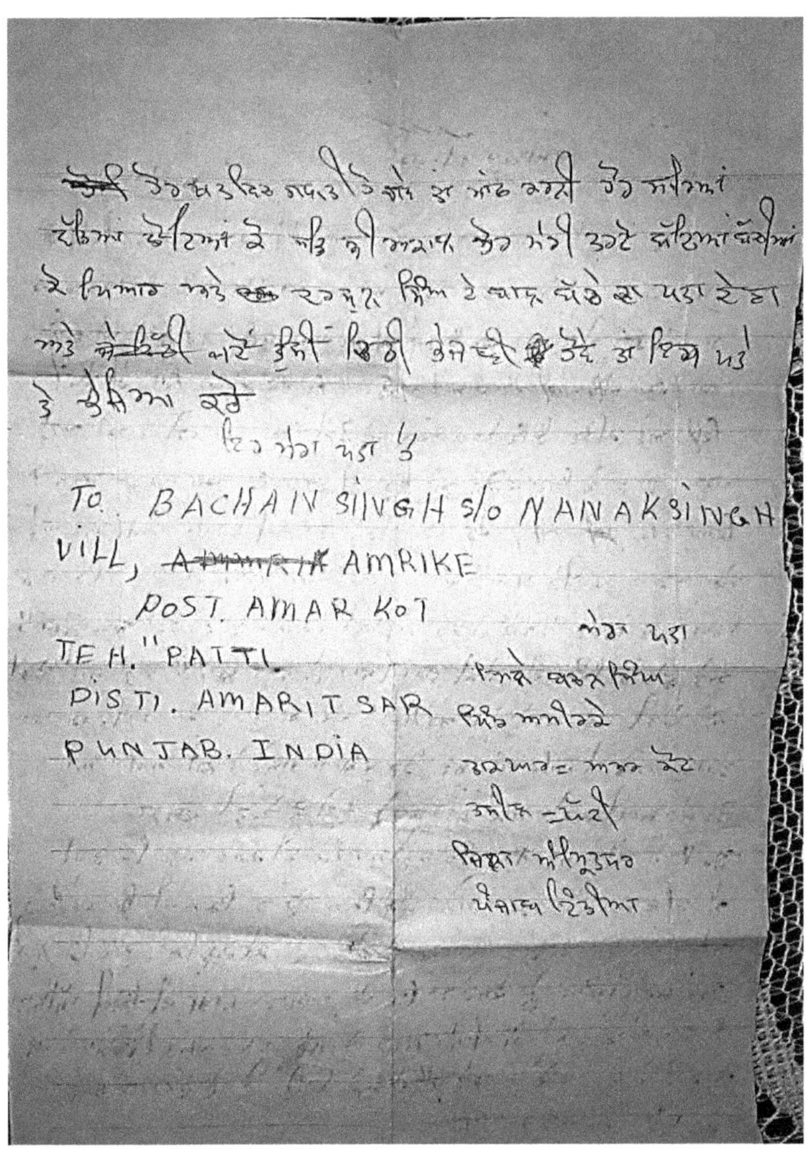

Letters from my grandfather to his brother, Bachan Singh in Amarkot. Our first real clue to solving the puzzle.

My grandparents at their wedding finery sometime in mid-1940 at Queens Street Gurdwarda. No wedding records, cards or certificates remain.

My veins course with excitement right now since we will be making our way to Valtoha tomorrow. I'll finally be able to see where you live and how you lived; perhaps even meet some old mates of yours or others who used to know you. Swing by places you used to hang out at or maybe even see the schoolyard where you flicked marbles on the sand. I'll finally be able to have an idea of some semblance of you apart from broken pieces of stories. Yes, I am dizzy with all these fantasies in my head. Also, I am somewhat equally aware that none of these may come to pass.

It's my birthday today, adding to the irony. Today, my family's celebrating my birth while we prepared to go and look for a dead man's story tomorrow. I never thought much for birthdays, seeing how celebrating the day I was born doesn't amount to much. I think that events, milestones and accomplishments are much more worthy of celebration. There's something very egotistical about celebrating a birthday. Yet, everyone does it. Honestly, I'm more excited about visiting your village tomorrow than celebrating the day I was born today.

We'd gone and spent the day in Amritsar. That beautiful golden temple where people come by the droves. It was gorgeous and we went and dipped in the waters. I'm not sure if it cleansed me to be honest. I am a product of my past, both good and bad. I almost don't want to be washed clean, but here we are. It's a thing to do and here we are actually doing it. We saw the grand hall and their kitchens but the rushing swine of a tour guide never quite let us enjoy it. It's such a place, though. The simultaneous grandeur and humility with the armed guards who wouldn't let me put my arm round my own mother for a picture. It all made me wonder where I was and what it truly meant. I never quite was truly Sikh. My father could never grow his hair out and when he tried, he'd fall ill. He never tried to grow my brother's and my hair out for fear of the same thing happening. My mother is Catholic and tried to raise my brother and I that way. We never quite aligned with her beliefs because my brother and I both found ourselves quite turned off by the ritualistic nature of Catholicism. We never really had strong faith in any religious belief for a large portion of our years growing up. In a long roundabout way, I became Buddhist during my time in Myanmar and eventually served a period of monkhood as well. We never quite caught onto Sikhism, as beautiful as its philosophy is. Yet, here I find myself in Amritsar, returning with long hair, no turban and lots of understandable stares from everyone.

I do wonder though, if you came to Amritsar often. I imagine that you visited the Golden Temple and the nearby marketplaces when you were younger. Grabbing street snacks and hanging out with friends by the red buildings that line either side of the marketplaces. Smiling and slapping your friends' backs every time a beautiful girl sauntered by, or you spotted someone out of town. I'm sure it was all a lot different back then but the main places are still here. I did imagine you standing where I stand, on the bank of the large pool, looking at the big block of gold in the middle; watching that unreachable, unattainable wisdom. That cruel, unfair prize so fairly and equally unreachable from all sides of the pool. Impossible to get to, save the one bridge that led directly to it.

I wonder if you were religious at all. You kept the traditions and practices of Sikhism but never made it so that your son should do the same. Alas, my turbanless, beardless father never raised us religious although we did visit temples and gurdwaras sometimes. Here I am today, just as turbanless and beardless as my father is. I wander the unforgiving streets of Amritsar with long hair but no turban, with a stubble but no beard. I wander the unforgiving streets of Amritsar unforgiven, unpardoned. How important is growing your hair out and having lands though, really? Could we not uphold the principles of Sikhism without these things to show?

Where does the modern Sikh come into play and should he be damned for not having the Five K's [6]?

Either way, I will discover something tomorrow. Tomorrow, the day will be that glue that pieces all the broken stories together. Tomorrow, everything will be clearer and I will see where ghosts had lived. I will turn you more human than you've ever been to me. My father will finally know more about his father. He'll be able to bring together bits of his puzzle and piece together his own broken stories. Together, we will turn a memory into something fleshier, more human, more paternal. Maybe these things will happen. Maybe, but realistically, probably not. The ridiculousness of it all suddenly dawned on me at the dinner table. The utter ridiculousness of searching for traces of a man who left in the 1940s, 80 years later. A shot in the dark at a needle in a haystack – the utterly impossible.

---

[6] The 5Ks Sikhism: *Kesh* (uncut body hair), *kangha* (a wooden comb), *kada* (an iron or steel bracelet), *kirpan* (a small curved dagger), and a *kachera* (a shorts-like undergarment).

Upon their arrival from Singapore, we all met up for the first time at Amritsar airport. The Indian Explorers (L to R): Nimmi John, Gabriela Minor, Manjit Singh and me.

Customer No.	Customer Name
1	Hamant Singh

Reservation details

Flight date	Departure / Arrival time	To / From	Flight
Tuesday 31 Jan 2023OBJT27CTGZMEX	09:42 PM / 11:30 PM	Tuxtla Gutiérrez, Tuxtla **(TGZ)** - Ciudad de México, Benito Juárez T1 **(MEX)**	Y4 795

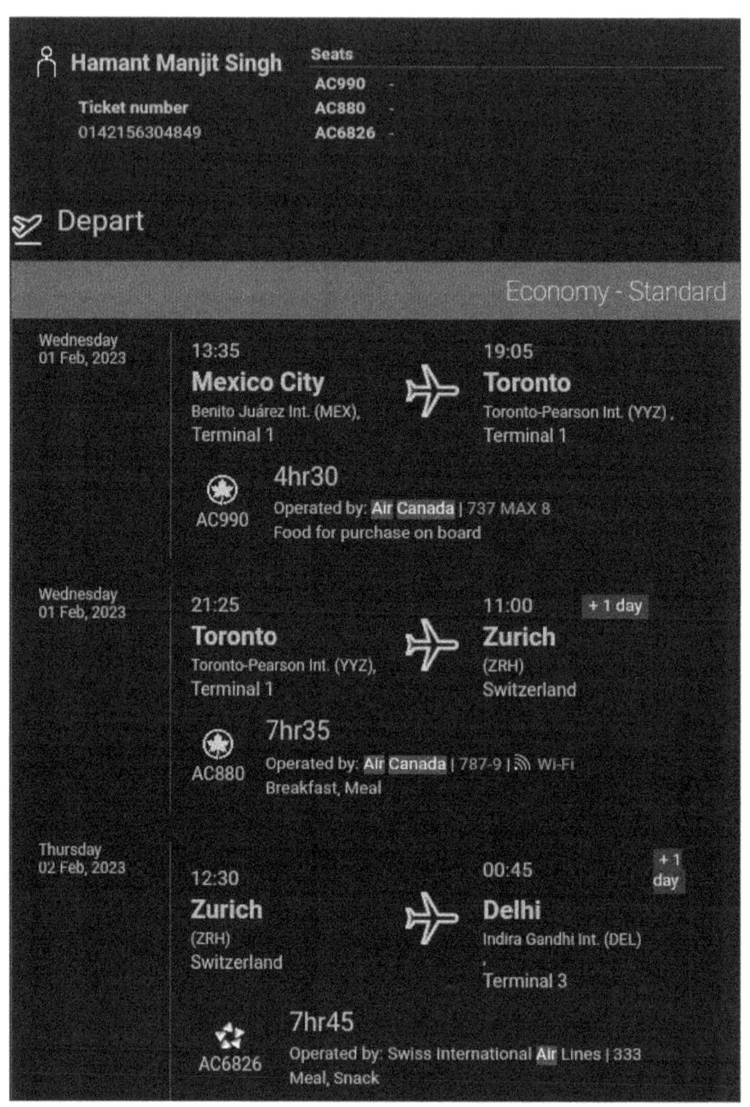

The incredibly long journey that began with a 14-hour layover in Mexico City. Over 36 hours of flying time before I finally arrived in Delhi.

We left the hotel early and made our way towards the most obvious place to begin. We started our search at the Post Office in Amarkot, situated outside Valtoha with no real address of its own and very little information in general. We definitely needed more if we were going to actually locate your village.

The hour-long car ride was a quiet affair, really. No one said much possibly because we all knew that there was very little chance of finding anything concrete. I imagined that our driver Deep Singh was probably thinking we were stark raving mad. City folk driving southwest to some godforsaken farming village with nothing more than a few pictures of a letter and a post office address. He was a smiley, cheerful fella with his moustache ends twisted up. What the hell did he care for? He was getting paid for the entire day, whether we found Valtoha or whether we found nothing.

It occurred to me that you probably would've driven down this same stretch of road but in the opposite direction, sometime in early 1940. I looked around and saw the same things that you saw. The landscape probably hasn't changed very much. Many things haven't really changed very much. Technological breakthroughs have allowed it so that I could come here and seek you out, but here there are still vast, open fields on both sides of the road. My father suddenly broke the silence, echoing what I just thought out loud. "My father would have been down this same road," he said with eyes not leaving his scan of the fields. I looked behind me from the passenger seat and smiled. I told him how I was literally just thinking the same thing. Many things haven't really changed very much. I am the son of your son, after all.

We took a quick stop at a gas station outside Amarkot for a bathroom break and a quick smoke. I think at this point, we were ready. You can imagine how we were all shaking with excitement and anticipation of the events to follow. We got back into the car and entered Amarkot. It wasn't long before we located the post office with the help of some toothless old men pointing the way. As we entered the dilapidated building, we drew the attention of everyone in the general vicinity. The state of the mail office gave the impression that mail got delivered on time in this part of the country. On the right, we found a little room with two men sitting idly inside. It appeared we had found Amarkot Post Office and its fine employees. My father then began asking the two men if they could help us locate your village. Although they were lounging lazily enough for 11 am on a Monday morning, they showed an ironic eagerness to lend us a hand. It was probably the most exciting thing

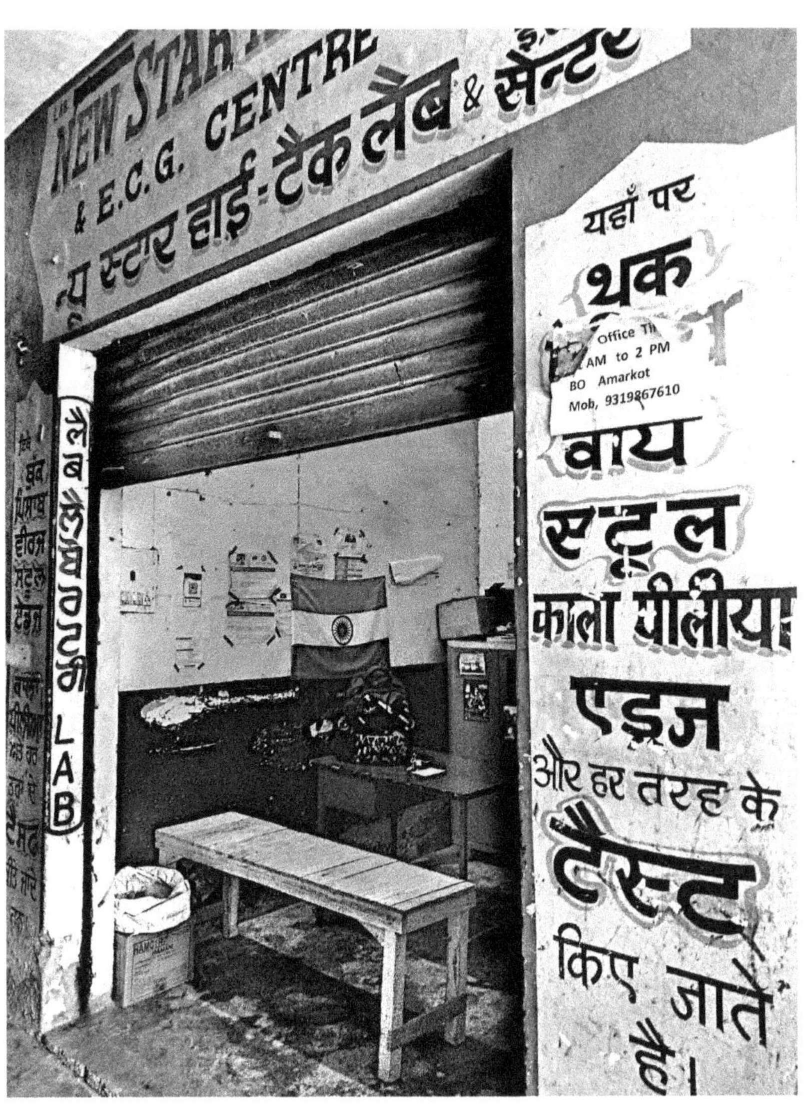
NEW STAR
& E.C.G. CENTRE
न्यू स्टार हाई-टेक लेब & सेन्टर
यहाँ पर
थक
Office Th
AM to 2 PM
BO Amarkot
Mob, 9319867610
वाय
स्टूल
काला गीलीया
एड्ज
और हर तरह के
टैस्ट
किए जाते
है
बल्डपैटरी
LAB

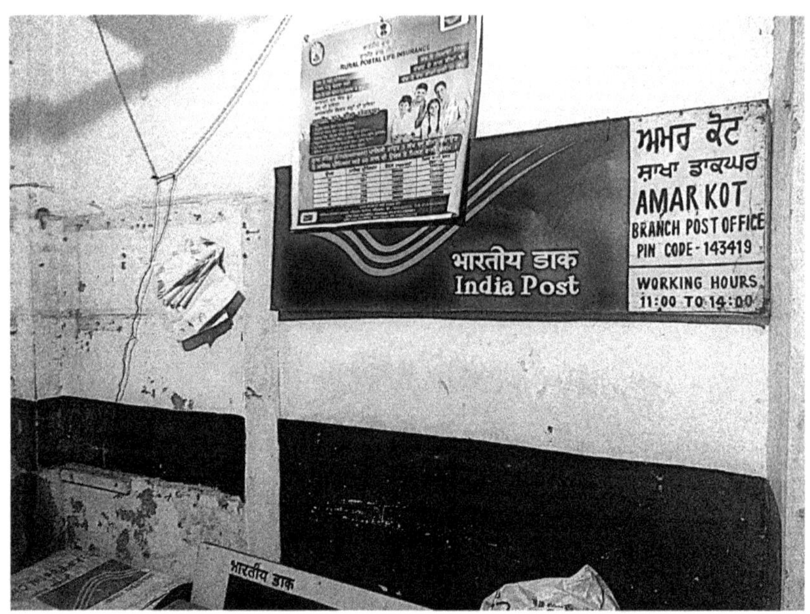

Front and inside shots of the tiny unit that is Amarkot Post Office. Strangely enough, no letters or parcels were found inside the unit.

to happen to them all month, judging by the look of the sleepy town. At this point I began to wonder what we were doing *not* being in Valtoha. I mean, that was the whole point wasn't it? I was convinced we were looking in the wrong place, but decided to stay quiet and see what would come of the enquiries here. It wasn't much that we had at this point but that we didn't have any better leads than this.

We were directed to an old timer in the pharmacy next door who began asking more questions. We showed him the letter and began telling him who we were and what we knew. His long white beard trembled gently as he asked us more about you and your brother, Bachan Singh. Clearly he was someone that was respected enough in the community. With his grand beard and his stature, it was quite hard to ignore his innate stately demeanour. We were asked what your caste was but we hadn't the slightest clue. We didn't know which clan you were from either or very much else apart from the information in the letter. To think that we've lived as long as we have without even knowing what caste you came from. I guess these things don't directly affect how we live these days where we are. Still, I think it would have mattered to you and your brothers. Things began to look bleak for us and the search until he decided to call the local *sarpanch*[7] of Amarkot.

This proved to be a breakthrough because he surely would have information of some kind that might help at least give us a smaller district to narrow our search. He could play a key role in locating the proverbial needle in the haystack. We were just waiting for him to arrive and I guess that meant tea time in India. We quickly found ourselves sitting by the side of the road with our tiny

---

[7] A *sarpanch* is the leader of a local village council (*panchayat*) that corresponds with the government.

little cups in our hands, just passing time. My mum
bought some oranges so that also kept us busy for a
while.

That's the thing about waiting though isn't it? The things
you do don't really matter but you're not actually waiting
if you're doing something. The things you do to pass
the time start to lose meaning if you consider it to be
waiting. Case in point, I suppose? I can't even
remember what we were talking about so we were
definitely waiting, just wasting moments. How I wish
there was something memorable so that I remember
that wait differently.

Then it happened out of an 'Amarkot' nowhere. A black,
shiny Audi pulled up some time later and out stepped a
tall, handsome man. Oh, how that Audi stood out from
the rest of the landscape! Traditionally, a *sarpanch*
would be an older member of the community but that
clearly wasn't the case here. Our latest aid was neither
old nor toothless but had the same kind, helpful
demeanour as our previous informants. A greeting left
his lips as promptly as he approached us with palms
pressed together. You would've been proud of how this
young *sarpanch* carried himself; new blood, new ideas.
He didn't lack for anything when it came to style either.
Simply dressed but in modern clothes, he naturally
drew attention everywhere he went. Perhaps, it was
admiration more than simply attention. Either way, he

definitely stood out amongst the rest, much like the way his car stood out on the street.

We didn't need to mention much more than Bachan Singh's name and the fact that he went to Singapore before we were flooded with much more information. He talked about how Bachan Singh's sons were all born in Singapore and had returned to Amarkot. He even knew where they lived in Singapore. That's right, your nephews are right there in Amarkot and we found them!

So this clearly left us all utterly confused since your last name was Valtoha. I imagined we would've needed to head back in the other direction since we just drove past Valtoha! Either way, we all got back into our hired car and followed the black Audi deeper into the countryside. If the Audi stood out like a sore thumb in the main street of Amarkot, just imagine what it looked like driving past the low swinging tails of cows and infinite acres and acres of open fields. After a few turns around dusty sand paths, the Audi came to a halt at a bend. It pulled up next to more cows and a pyramid of cow dung cakes piled on top of each other. We looked at each other and it appeared that we had come home.

~

The house was a humble affair, with many rooms built

with brick walls. To add to the confusion, we were told that Bachan Singh's house was next to this one and the people who now lived in it were still in the main town. It was locked right now but we would be able to see it later. Something about this particular house felt unfinished but clearly there had been people living there for some time. Slowly, two men emerged from the house, dressed in very simple kurtas with cloths hastily wrapped around their heads. One was slightly serious-looking while the other was smiling incessantly. Two ladies brought plastic chairs out for us to sit and the young *sarpanch* explained who we were. As if on cue, both their heads turned towards us. *Dadaji*, these two men are your nephews, Teja Singh and Ranjit Singh. Tears filled Ranjit Singh's eyes even though he was still smiling. The look on Teja Singh's face, on the other hand, was a mix of joy and horror.

We were invited to sit down for a bit of a chat with some samosas and tea. It was mostly my father talking really since the rest of us had basically zero Punjabi or Hindi. At the end of snack time, we were each handed a small glass of milk. While my father downed it easily enough, my mother, Gaby and I were left gagging and struggling to drink any of it. It was clearly a Punjabi thing that didn't survive the generations. The milk was thick beyond what I knew as 'full cream'. Punjabis believe that it gives them strong bones and this is probably the reason they end up as large and strong as they do.

Front entrance to the first house we entered belonged to Teja Singh (foreground) and Ranjit Singh (inside at the time) and their families.

We were then brought out back to see the fields. My dad asked the brothers which plots belonged to them. "As far as your eyes can see," was Teja Singh's response. They mostly grew wheat or atta[8] as it's known in the region. They were also growing a bit of sugarcane and they brought us to see the crops.

There was an air about them as they were as they walked through the fields. It was almost as if they were displaying their wealth and their pride. It suddenly dawned upon me that our family must've belonged to the *Jat*[9] caste. Judging from the general state of the area, you must've been raised in an agrarian setting. This probably also explains why you worked so hard, why your son does and why I do. I never quite favoured luck in life over hard work. These vast, open fields that lie before me, and the pride on your nephews' faces are testament enough to that ethic running through our bloodline.

At this point, we still didn't know what we were doing in Amarkot, or what they were doing there for that matter. Who was living there anyway, who were these people "still in the main town"? As far as I was concerned we were wasting too much time here and needed to check out Valtoha, whatever was there. It turns out that truths were indeed unravelling. But like the progress, politics and police work in India, it was taking its own sweet time.

---

[8] Wheat grown in the region is then used to make *chapatis,* flat bread that is a staple in Punjabi cuisine.
[9] A north Indian caste that predominantly deals with agriculture.

We were then taken in another direction and shown the family gurdwara. They actually had an entire gurdwara of their own! Despite the shabby condition that the house was in, these people clearly had money and were prominent enough in the community. Everyone called out to them as we walked by different houses. Also, if the *sarpanch* and the old man from the pharmacy knew who they were, they must be important enough.

~

After our little tour of the fields, Teja Singh said his brother was on the way back from town. Clearly he was the one currently living in Bachan Singh's house. We made our way through little alleyways that led to the other house. This time, its gates were wide open and they were expecting us. As we entered, there was a small building on the right that was covered with tarp. They seemed eager to show us something and began tearing the tarp off. They explained that this little building was the first thing Bachan Singh had built when he arrived back from Singapore. They were peeling piece after piece of tarp that eventually revealed a small building that had been turned into a cowshed. A cow and its calf were just standing around inside this little piece of history. On the top, were the still visible words painted that read: "Bachan Singh 1967".

Background: Ranjit Singh, my father and Teja Singh. Three of their grandchildren are in the foreground.

We moved to sit in the veranda with more sugary drinks while we chatted with Teja Singh and Ranjit Singh. It was still my father doing most of the talking while we listened and tried to glean as much as we could. Halfway through the conversation, Teja Singh told Ranjit to do something and our gaze followed as he stood up. He walked over to a rusty tap on the side and filled a bucket with some water. With a half-smile still dangling on his face, he walked over to where a cow and calf were tied. With his back to us, he slid his fingers down the cow's udders. He seemed to have been warming it up for the calf that he brought to feed right after. Ranjit tapped the calf's hide as it greedily suckled them and then turned to face us with a huge smile on his face.

As power plays were beginning to show themselves, a man with bright golden shoes and a yellow turban suddenly arrived on the scene with a black plastic bag. On his right was an excited-looking woman, smiling from ear to ear with a proper skip in her step. It was almost reminiscent of a king entering his court. He seemed to be a larger, life-sized version of The Sultan from Aladdin, corpulence dressed in opulence. It wasn't just his attire but the way everyone almost bowed as he entered the space. He basically pranced through the entrance towards our direction; a king entering his court. I think we all noticed the change in atmosphere on some level as my family exchanged quick glances; communicating without words. Things were definitely beginning to get more interesting in this tiny town.

Ripping off the tarp on the small shed. This was the first building on the compound.

They were introduced to us as Kirpal Singh and his wife, and he began telling us that they had all been born in Singapore. So now we knew his name but clearly not who he truly was. He rummaged around the black bag and whipped out its only contents: two Singaporean identity cards. These were older Singaporean identity cards from the 50s and 60s. I only know this because I had once seen an older ID that belonged to my maternal grandmother. I had to admit, they were in pristine condition for IDs that were about 60 years old. The lamination definitely ensured they kept well and most details were still very legible. I grabbed them, laid them out and started taking pictures of the first bit of actual family history we had found so far. For the first time, I was able to see what your brother and his wife Harbans Kaur looked like; able to put faces to nameless ghosts. She had shortened her name to Bans Kaur but he kept the 'son of' (S/O) Nanak Singh in his official name. We sat around a little longer before we moved indoors and this was when revelations were made.

~

The interior of this second house looked a lot more finished than the previous one we were in. A picture of your brother seemed to oversee the entire house, hung close to the entrance of your house. Settling slowly into their seats, they began talking to us about you, *Dadaji*. We all sat around a small table as Kirpal's wife eagerly brought out some old school records and photo albums. The former belonged to one of their older sisters and contained her early primary school records. She had been a student at Selegie Primary School on Short Street, which strangely enough was the same school my father had gone to. I'm guessing your brother and you had both put your children in the school closest to where you had lived. Convenience, I imagine, while you both slogged away to provide for the family. I suppose any education in a Singaporean school was going to be better than that in Valtoha or Amarkot, for that matter.

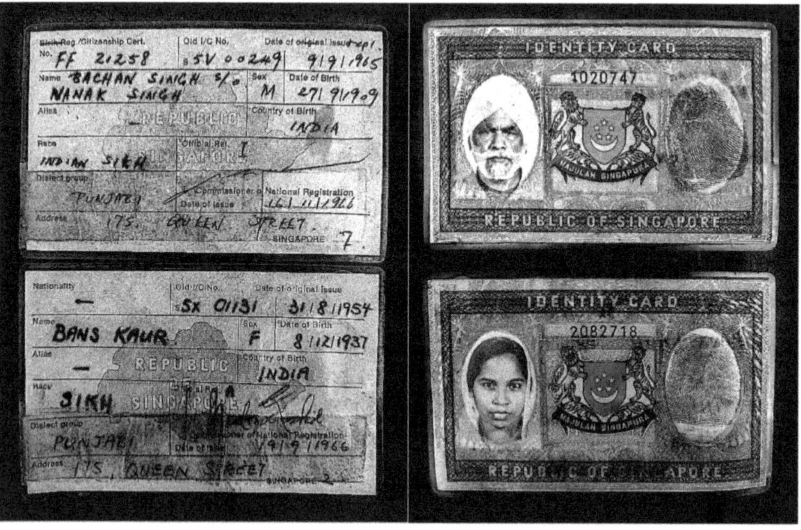

Identity cards belonging to my granduncle and grandaunt. Their alleged dates of birth are on it and so was their address.

While the school records contained little new information, the same cannot be said of the photo albums. There were old pictures of your brother, his wife and many others of the both of you. We also found shots of the younger versions of the three brothers and their sisters. In one of the albums, I saw a picture of you. A young *Jat* atop a tractor, completely oblivious to the fact that you were being photographed. You looked so proud with your turban carelessly wrapped around your head. I looked at the picture and saw a man of the soil, hard at work. Hard work seemed to define you whichever way I looked at it. You would've been glad that this character trait went on to define your son and his sons after him. There were also pictures of your wife, my *Dadiji* in the prime of her youth. She sat there, a regal beauty with piercing eyes next to her sister. In other pictures, we saw her photographed with my father as a baby sat on her lap.

While I was busy photographing the pictures in the album, the three brothers began narrating a story to my father. While I was busy capturing memories, they began to set free caged secrets of betrayal and deceit. "We're surprised to see you here. We thought you were all dead," Kirpal began. Despite my limited Punjabi, I turned my attention towards the old storyteller. His jolly demeanour had taken a very serious turn. "When your father died, Bachan Singh had returned to Singapore to

look for your mother and her children. When he failed to
find them, he returned to Amarkot and told us that
everyone we knew in Singapore was dead," Kirpal
Singh said. My father smiled and responded almost too
quickly, "I remember when Bachan Singh came to
Singapore after my father's accident. He was going to
bring us all back to India and my mother didn't want
that. When she found out Bachan Singh had returned,
she hid all of us for a few days." Your son paused and
laughed a little, "Somehow, he got what he wanted in a
way. Here we are!"

My father's lighter mood didn't sit as well with them. The
three brothers didn't really see the humour in my
father's words and exchanged nervous looks. They
went on to explain what had happened in Valtoha.
When your oldest brother, Tara Singh, had sold
everything in Valtoha, he tricked both Bachan Singh and
you. He left you both a small amount of money, with
which you both fled to Singapore. They all agreed that
Tara Singh was a conniving person who apparently had
no mercy, not even for his brothers. My father recalled
his mother also mentioning that my granduncle wasn't a
very nice person. This was all strange to me, though.
Hearing your son and nephews talk about my
granduncle, your brother Tara Singh, who seems to
have somehow managed to make enough enemies for
someone who was deaf and mute.

"This is your house!" interjected an excited Kirpal Singh.
Teja Singh didn't say anything but nodded, not so much
in agreement as much as concession. Ranjit on the
other hand, was still all smiles. In some ways, it really
was ours because they knew what had happened and
how Bachan Singh had enough money to come back
and buy this large expanse of land. We were told that
he bought the land when he had returned to Amarkot.
Yes, Amarkot not Valtoha. He probably didn't return to
Valtoha since everything they owned had been sold and
Tara Singh was dead. The truth was that there was
nothing to return to in Valtoha. Where the rest of the
money was seemed doomed to be yet another mystery
on the already long list; not that we truly cared where it
was. It had all become crystal clear to us that we were
in Amarkot and not Valtoha because there was literally
no trace at all of them there.

It seems your brother and you went through quite a bit
of betrayal at the hands of Tara Singh. It wasn't
explicitly mentioned, but it seems that Bachan Singh
had left you in the lurch as well. You were in a situation
where your six children and wife were now
fundamentally your responsibility. Responsibility you
had to take on with little to no financial backing. All you
had was your work ethic. Since it was never brought up,
we all thought it best to let some truths rest with those
that have been laid to rest. Too many truths had been
unearthed that day and we could almost sense the

need to stop digging. In hindsight, your hard work is the only real reason that we were able to make it back to this country and uncover truths about you. Not specifically Valtoha, but important truths nonetheless.

At this juncture Balvinder Singh, Teja Singh's son, entered the room. Even more animated than his father and armed with some English, he proceeded to introduce himself and talk to us. He expressed how happy he was to see us and that he had been to Singapore himself. We then engaged in some small talk, quite happy that we had some common ground

My grandfather and grandmother in individual photographs, as seen in the photo albums they showed us in Amarkot.

My Dadaji, on a tractor back in Valtoha. This photo is from the 1930s in Valtoha, long before he even considered a move to Singapore.

and a more common tongue. He went on and on about his time in Singapore, how happy he was to see us and how excited he was that his "blood" had returned.

Something possessed Kirpal Singh at this point to turn to my father and ask him for his sandals. Your son, being the humble man that he is, explained how his sandals were old and that he meant to buy new ones. After repeated refusals, my father caved and gave in.

LEFT: My grandmother and her sister 'Billy', which is Punjabi for cat. She got that nickname because her eyes were blue.

RIGHT: Sat in the middle is my grandmother with a very young Manjit Singh (my father) on her lap. 'Billy' is standing on her right.

Kirpal removed his golden shoes and offered them in exchange. My father accepted it, albeit hesitantly I imagine, while we watched intently by the sidelines, in a great deal of confusion. My father then went on to remove his watch and gifted it to Kirpal, an action which throttled the turbaned cousin to new levels of excitement. What he did next was unthinkable and left us all absolutely floored. He removed his sandals and put them on top of his turban[10]! You could hear a pin drop as everyone watched the maharaja cede his crown to the visiting foreigners. I couldn't help but wonder if this was a calculated political move or a genuine display of surrender. My father however, was clearly faking smiles of comfort in Kirpal Singh's shoes. Golden shoes and glamour never did fit your son anyway.

~

Suddenly, the younger girls in the family called out to Gaby as the rest of us wondered what was going on. Although we weren't married at the time, we had to tell them that we'd been married for a year. I cannot imagine the chaos that would ensue if they found out that we'd been living together as an unmarried couple for years. In my defence, I had proposed a few days later at the Taj Mahal so the lie was really quite short-lived.

We then went on to exchange telephone numbers as we finished our cups of tea. When we casually mentioned that we had to leave, we were met with a swift wave of refusal. They offered to pay Deep Singh

---

[10] A Sikh's turban is the ultimate symbol of their identity, pride, spirituality and honour. It should never be touched by another, removed or disrespected in any way or form. One's shoes on the other hand are seen as unclean objects since you wear them whilst stepping on all sorts of things on the street.

and insisted that we spent our remaining days at "our house". My father declined politely saying that I needed to go back to the hotel and clock work hours on the computer at the hotel. The truth is that it was all quite overwhelming for us and the day had brought more than enough hospitality. These people were warm but I think we were dizzy enough from the revelations for the day. It was perhaps more probable that your son, and his son, needed a good long smoke and a tall whiskey to properly process all that had just happened.

All of this didn't sit too well with Kirpal Singh who promptly whipped his phone out and dialled the *sarpanch* directly. He told him that we were planning to leave and the *sarpanch* joined in the protests. He offered to bring his laptop to the house so I could work and he would stay with us all. As an alternative, he also suggested that we spend the night at his place and dined as guests. They were doing everything in their power to make us stay longer than we planned to. The more cynical side of me couldn't help but wonder if it was more than just 'good ol' country hospitality'. There was a nagging instinctual feeling that there was perhaps something more sinister afoot. We were humbled but once again politely declined; my work security and associated permissions being the reason cited for our necessary departure. This time, we were successful since they'd exhausted every option to keep us there in Amarkot. We stood up and proceeded to take their leave.

As I moved toward the open doorway, Kirpal Singh's wife came towards me and pushed some money into my hand. She couldn't stop hugging me and once again her eyes welled up with tears. At this point, my very un-Punjabi mother stood up and started handing out money as well. This almost minister-like distribution of money paved the way for our exit, eventually to where Deep Singh was parked. Thankfully, we followed her out to the driveway where Gaby was returned to us. The girls of the house had absconded a confused Mexican and had returned a girl, more shaken than a margarita. She re-joined our group looking stunned, and quite eager to return to the hotel. I guess my father and I weren't the only ones who needed a drink! Ranjit Singh came to me and gave me some money as well. The money he had given me was accompanied with his usual smile and a very warm hug. It really impressed me that he, who seemed to be the least important of the three brothers, managed to give me a little something. This gesture meant more to me than what the others had given me. Clearly, this distribution of money was a common sending-off tradition in Punjab.

Indeed, the eventful day and the Punjabi sun had taken a lot out of us. All four of us got in the car feeling dizzy and drunk. I remember looking out the window after shutting the doors and seeing them all line up. The ecstatic goodbyes in their waves and on their lips oddly seemed simultaneously relieving and contrived. After discovering the history of the brothers and what they were like, it was as if the hospitality and goodbyes masked something greater, something darker. The ride back was sombre, to say the least and there was a general silence in the car. Perhaps it was being overwhelmed, or perhaps it was sheer exhaustion from the day and what it brought.

After we'd all had a shower, we gathered in my parents' hotel room and evaluated the day. Personally, I was content with finding out that Valtoha and Amarkot were more than just signboards and fables. Everything else that happened today was an absolute bonus, even though it avalanched upon us in the way that it did.

Seeing all that we had needed to see, we headed back toward Amritsar. Shortly after leaving Amarkot, we passed some town called Valtoha, whatever that town is.

It's our last day in Punjab before we head to Kashmir tomorrow. We decided to pay the Golden Temple another visit before heading back to finish some half-opened bottles and pack our things.

While we were too exhausted to sit about and chat last night, tonight was quite a different story. My mother and Gaby joined in as we all sat and talked about Amarkot and its colourful characters. Apart from the obvious events of the day, we really wanted to know what happened when Gaby was abducted by the other girls and what they had done. She sent us into a fit of laughter, talking about how they dressed her and made her up. They had spent the rest of the time taking pictures with the Mexican who they probably thought was Indian. Correcting them, explaining where she was from and how we met would've been too much trouble. In many ways, she would've been just as foreign with whichever nationality she had chosen for the day.

She went along with it since she was confused and it all seemed harmless anyway. To say she was traumatised may be a tad dramatic, but I think on some level, we didn't have too much of an idea what was going on ourselves throughout the day. There was also so much fogginess about who some of the wives, husbands, sons and daughters truly belonged to. However, some things were crystal clear and our observations were somehow quite unanimous.

For them, seeing us return from Singapore was probably a lot like watching the dead come back to life. They must've imagined that we were there for land that belonged to us; land that Tara Singh and Bachan Singh had tricked you out of. We all felt an initial discomfort, an awkward air when we had arrived. We hadn't come for the land although we clearly had a claim to it. Realistically, it's not like we were going to leave our lives and jobs behind and work the lands in the way they need to be worked. We don't even know the first thing about farming! We could all also see how they began to ease up after they had realised that we just wanted to learn more about our family and our history. We were visibly more excited about pictures and stories than knowing the size of the fields. If they had decided otherwise, we very well might've been greeted with a rifle.

It was also pretty obvious who was in charge of the entire operation. Kirpal Singh was in town when we arrived and we saw his influence over everyone when he returned. Teja Singh seemed to be the most responsible of the lot, but also the most reserved. He was a man of few words and usually only spoke when spoken to. Ranjit Singh was clearly the stooge. Seeing how he was the darkest of the three, he probably spent the most time out in the fields. We guessed that he didn't complain much and just did what he was told. He didn't appear to be the sharpest tool in the shed, but that's what he had his brothers for. Still, both brothers needed Ranjit Singh to perform the simpler, more hands-on tasks. They needed him to spend the hours that he did, tending to crops and cows and working the land. They needed him to do the more laborious work and he did it, with a smile on his face the whole time.

Another one we talked about was Balvinder Singh, who had been texting me the entire day. I tried to be as polite as possible but really didn't want to speak to him. Not because I had something against him but I had nothing to say to him, really. I told my father how I thought his dramatic verbal performance before we left the house was a bit over the top. While everyone felt the same, my father pointed out that he had acted that way out of worry. In my head, it was clear that we weren't there for the property. So what was it, then? My father went on to explain how both Ranjit Singh and Teja Singh had daughters and Kirpal Singh was the only one with a son. This meant that he would be the sole inheritor of everything when my father's cousins passed. Being as young as he is, he probably couldn't figure out that we hadn't come for anything but to see them. In his eyes, we were still a threat. This probably explains why he was texting me, still wanting to keep in contact in case we were planning a legal assault after the visit.

Some years ago, two of my father's sisters had gone in search of Valtoha and found it. They hopped on a bus from Amritsar and did indeed arrive there. Naturally, they didn't find family or any other details particularly relevant to you or your brothers. Up to that point in time, that was the closest any of us had come to finding you and our little team here hadn't even thought about coming at the time. It still feels like we had accomplished quite the feat. My mother and Gaby didn't think we would find anything either and I couldn't blame the lack of faith. To walk into a town in Singapore, say Punggol or Tampines, and ask around for a person's name seemed ridiculous. And this was India! What chance did we realistically have? If it wasn't for the bearded man in the pharmacy and the *sarpanch* helping out, we would've quite easily gone home empty handed.

Gaby was starting to feel dizzy, either from the whiskey or revisiting the experience, or both! She headed off to bed when she had had enough and was done for the night. My mother lay in bed, in and out of sleep, while my father and I continued with whiskey and conversation. One of the things he'd brought up was the death of your first daughter. I was told that you had a daughter who was with you when you worked at the soap factory. The story goes that she'd slipped and fell into one of the soap vats while running and playing. I had never heard of this first aunt of mine till today and wondered why something so significant was never mentioned ever. Jugjit Kaur was her name, another family secret who didn't have the time to develop into a ghost. It indeed appears the deeper I dig, the more secrets and skeletons I unearth.

Perhaps this is it, our family. We're reluctant to talk about ghosts, or to ghosts or even to address them. I suppose my letters to you have gone against that tradition; or perhaps, it was subconscious rebellion borne out of it. So much for a search for family resulting in the defiance of traditions. There's something quite melancholic and beautiful in the silence surrounding the dead. Do we honour their memory by not speaking of them? Seems like a strange way to remember them or perhaps, the goal is to forget them. They don't serve much purpose anymore since they are no longer with us. It almost feels wrong, taboo even, to discover more about those that have gone before. Clearly, we do 'remember' them by slinging garlands round black and white faded photographs; slinging lassos around fleeting memories. However, to do anything more than that somehow feels prohibited. It may well be that you were kept such a secret because this is the way the family honoured the dead. Maybe you never were a ghost but you were made out to be.

I've decided to chronicle this little adventure and turn it into a little book. After talking to friends and family, I've decided it best to immortalise you in this way. I began this process of finding you with more than enough silence and secrecy surrounding you. It really shouldn't have been this hard to find out more about my grandfather. However, it truly has been quite the ride, and here I find myself with more information than I began with. I still don't even know your favourite colour, your favourite dish or your pastimes. With the little that I do have, I'm going to try and publish our correspondence. We can't quite call it that since the communication has only been one-way. Still, I imagine your replies, the wisdom in your responses even though I find myself with rather empty hands. With these same empty hands, I'll still write what I want to, and in the process, speak about you. No more ghosts, no more disappearing, *Dadaji*; I've caught you and it is high time everyone knew about you. I feel like this is something you deserve, whether you wanted this or not.

There's so much missing from the story, I'll admit. I know you passed in an accident, but what actually happened? My search for more details found me writing to the Khalsa Association in Singapore and the National Archives for information about your accident. Neither had direct information, but both were kind enough to point me in the correct direction. I then ended up searching on the National Archives site with keywords. Searching for what exactly, I don't know; I used names, dates and any information I could muster in several different combinations. Then, I found an article about you, then another. I finally found you.

There's a story written about your crash, with another follow-up article two years later. Someone found that your story was important enough to be published and here we reap the fruits of the internet. I finally have a date when you passed. The article also details that *Dadiji* sued the guy who hit you. Turns out you weren't even in a vehicle. Upon texting my father, I found out that you were on the way to pick up your vehicle that you drove your boss around in. You had been walking safely on the pavement when one S. Chinnasamy lost control of his vehicle and mounted the curb. He hit you so hard that he managed to launch you into the Bukit Timah canal that ran next to the street. The authorities were unable to retrieve your body until four hours later when the water level dropped. All of this is of course very tragically poetic; launched out of our lives and a pain to recover. I also thought it was really ironic how it was another road vehicle that ended your life as you were on your way to the vehicle that provided for your livelihood.

They couldn't even spell your name right in the article, but then again, they didn't get your age right, did they? My father had told me that you had lied about your age to get citizenship. I think this was a common practice back in the day so now no one really knows how old you were. I suppose you did what you had to do but it was your undoing. They calculated the damages based on your age and how much longer you could've worked. 180 dollars a month was your monthly wage. Seems a pittance these days but it must've been everything to your family at the time. My brother and I spend that easily when we have a night out in present-day Singapore. *Dadiji* was a homemaker so you were pretty much the only source of income at the time.

They say she was hysterical when she arrived on the scene, and rightfully so. The article doesn't say much about her or your children, as the nature of reporting may have been at the time. I wonder what was worse: the sorrow in hearing how you had passed or the worry about how on earth she was going to raise five children. Still, a $17,000 cash out must've done loads to help with raising the children.

Fatal hit flings man into a canal

Shy S'poreans told: Smile to visitors

SINGAPORE, Friday

SHY Singaporeans were told today to emerge from their shells — for the sake of the country's tourism.

NTUC adviser Mr. Gerald de Cruz told 60 airport staff at the Paya Lebar airport: "We Asians are a naturally shy people. But in the context of your duties in Singapore, shyness has no place. Hosts cannot be shy."

Mr. de Cruz, who said he was speaking on behalf of NTUC secretary-general Mr. C.V. Devan Nair, was addressing representatives of the staff of airlines, Customs, Immigration and Health, and the Department of Civil Aviation, at the first meeting of the newly-formed NTUC Courtesy Campaign Committee.

The committee was formed yesterday with the immediate objective of stressing the importance of courtesy and politeness to

LEFEVRE, A 'BRITISH SUBJECT IN AUSTRALIA'

SINGAPORE, Fri. — The Ministry of Home Affairs today clarified its statement yesterday that an Australian tourist, Mr.

A PEDESTRIAN went flying into the air and plunged fatally into Bukit Timah canal after he was struck by a car, this morning.

The car ended smack into a lamp post, its driver critically injured.

It happened as contract driver Shangara Singh, 51, was walking to work in Bukit Timah Road near Rex cinema at about 7.30 a.m.

According to police the car, driven by S. Chinnasamy, 22, went out of control and knocked down Shangara who was on the footpath.

The impact was so great, Shangara was "catapulted" over the three-foot high iron railing of the swollen canal.

The body was stuck in the mud under eight feet of muddy water, and it was not until the water level fell about four hours later that police managed to recover it.

Shangara's widow rushed to the scene at about that time, wept hysterically and collapsed into the arms of relatives and friends. — Straits Times picture.

Council of Law Soci

LAWYER Mr. O. Starforth Hill has been re-elected president of the Council of the Law Society of Singapore for 1971 — a year which promises to be "extra-challenging."

The Council represents the interest of 300 members of the Singapore Bar.

Mr. H. L. Wee is the vice-president. The other members are Messrs. D. Murphy, A. P. Godwin, Karthigesu, S. W. Hancroft, J. B. Jeyaretnam, P. B. Menon, Wong Keon and Chan Kian Hin.

The Council will be

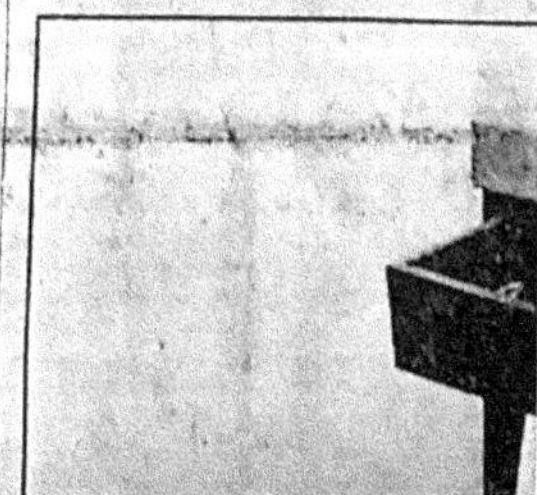

Pictures from the article that ran in The Straits Times (9th January 1971, pg 7)[11]

[11] https://eresources.nlb.gov.sg/newspapers/Digitised/Page/straitstimes197 10109-1.1.7

Article from the Eastern Sun (9th January 1971, pg 3)[12] that shows my grandfather's body being dragged out of the canal 4 hours after the accident had happened.

---

[12] https://eresources.nlb.gov.sg/newspapers/Digitised/Search?ST=1&AT=search&k=skidding%20car%20flings%20pedestrian#

Justice? At least there was some semblance of justice, I think. It doesn't really help our relationship since even ten times that amount wouldn't allow me to meet you. The compensation only really made up for so much but some things are beyond dollars and cents. What am I to do with an old newspaper article and spent compensation? What were your children to do with a missing father? I have no doubt that you and I would've gotten on really well. I would've wanted to be with you and sit with you. To tell you about the struggles today and what I've done and the things that I was going to do. I suppose I am, through these letters to you; letters to a ghost. Although, I admit that you're less of a ghost now; less of a ghost and more of an actual person.

I wonder what could've been if the crash didn't happen and if you had lived on. Would you have gone back to Punjab and settled there? I doubt it. I think you realised that you had built a new life now and Singapore is now the place you would've called 'home'. You would've visited at some point, no doubt. Visited probably just to see what became of Valtoha; what became of Amarkot and the family that lived there. Your nephews and nieces, their lives and their children's lives. Lives that have gone on without you in the picture but with the same agrarian setting.

There's a texting chat group now of all those that remain of your bloodline, those that have married and those that have moved elsewhere. Your daughters, their children and their spouses all pop something in the chat from time to time. We talk about memories and developments, befores and afters. We simultaneously reminisce, share our present endeavours and plan for the future.

This will be the last letter I write to you. There's no sense in writing to you nor a need for it any longer. It's like a cat chasing its tail, a dead tiger looking at its stripes, a grandson trying to understand his grandfather. The search is done and the enquiry is over. Maybe it all doesn't truly matter in the grand scheme of things, but it mattered to me. I went and searched and now I will tell the world about you, about where you came from and what it looks like now. Obviously, I wasn't there to say goodbye to you and no one was. The way you passed was so quick, wild and unpredictable. Strangely, this is all very much the way I've always lived my life. I think it's time now to lay you to rest - the memory of you and your story. I've tried to write this the best I can and perhaps, I may have faltered. There must have been more but I am content with what I have discovered. I just hope I've done justice to you and the story of your life. Goodbye *Dadaji*. I love you.

Waheguruji ka Khalsa, Waheguruji ki Fateh.

Miscellaneous Photographs and Documents

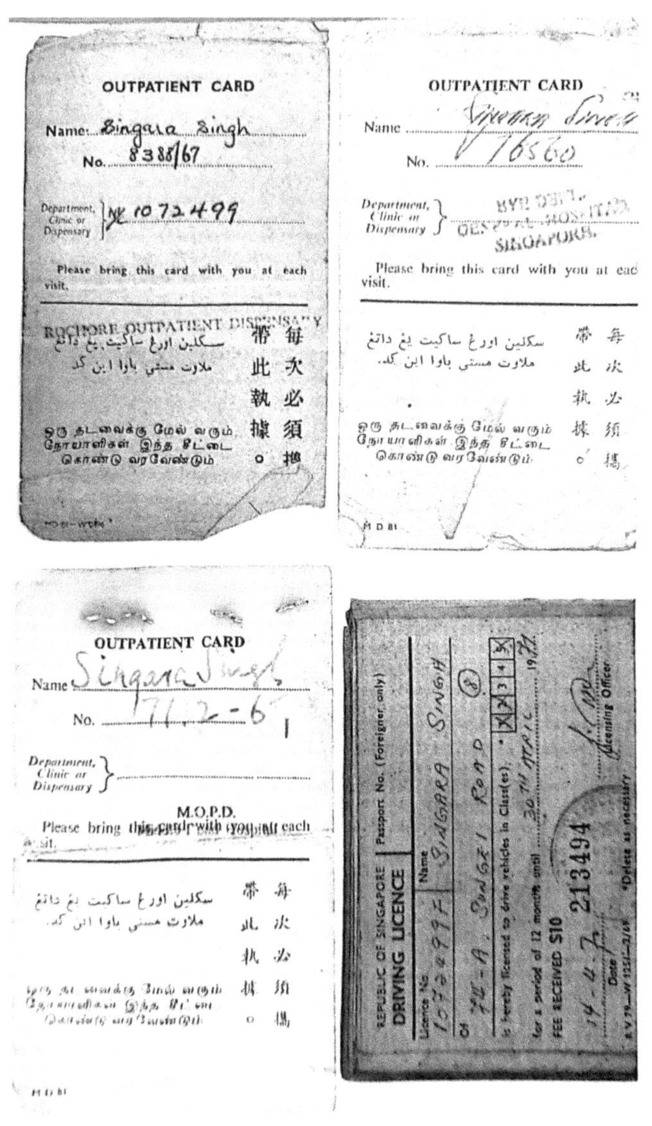

*Personal artefacts of my grandfather: An outpatient card
from Singapore General Hospital and his driver's licence.*

My grandfather's death certificate, issued the day after the fatal accident. It was collected by his daughter, Ajit Kaur. It sadly shows that he actually drowned to death and that the impact of the crash wasn't the immediate cause of death.

In the foreground, Teja Singh (left) speaks to the sarpanch and my father (far right). In the background is Deep Singh, our driver for the day. This photo was taken when we had just arrived at the residence.

L to R: Gabriela, me, Ranjit Singh, Ranjit Singh's wife, Nimmi, Manjit, Teja Singh, the man from the pharmacy and the sarpanch.

Boys in the front yard with lots to catch up on. L to R: Manjit, Teja and Ranjit.

Left: Photo of Bachan Singh that hangs in the living room of his house. The date in the picture indicates that he passed on 11th September 1984, two years before I was born.

The exterior (above) and interior (below) of the family gurdwara. This building is located behind their houses and is usually locked. This building is reserved for family use only.

Front yard of Bachan Singh's house. This section was built much later after the initial small front section of the house. Clearly, they built more as their wealth grew.

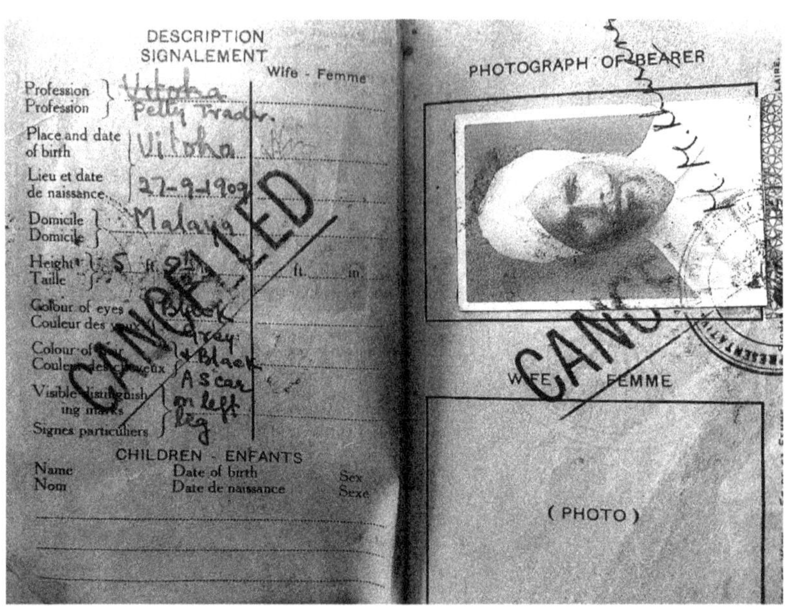

DESCRIPTION
SIGNALEMENT
Wife - Femme
Profession }
Profession }
Petty Trader
Place and date
of birth
Vitoha
Lieu et date
de naissance
27-9-1909
Domicile }
Domicile }
Malaya
Height }
Taille }
5 ft. 2 in.
Colour of eyes
Couleur des yeux
Black
Grey
Colour of hair
Couleur des cheveux
Black
Visible distinguish-
ing marks
Signes particuliers
A scar
on left
leg
CHILDREN - ENFANTS
Name   Date of birth   Sex
Nom   Date de naissance   Sexe
CANCELLED
PHOTOGRAPH OF BEARER
WIFE   FEMME
(PHOTO)
CANCELLED

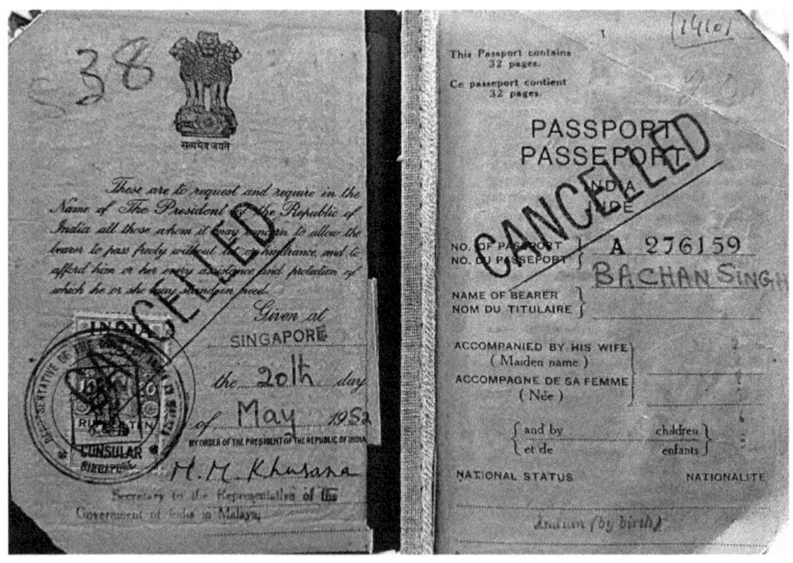

38
These are to request and require in the
Name of The President of the Republic of
India all those whom it may concern to allow the
bearer to pass freely without let or hindrance, and to
afford him or her every assistance and protection of
which he or she may stand in need.

Given at
SINGAPORE
the 20th day
of May 1952

BY ORDER OF THE PRESIDENT OF THE REPUBLIC OF INDIA

M. M. Khusana
Secretary to the Representative of the
Government of India in Malaya.

INDIA
CONSULAR
SINGAPORE
CANCELLED

This Passport contains
32 pages.
Ce passeport contient
32 pages.

PASSPORT
PASSEPORT
INDIA
DE

CANCELLED

NO. OF PASSPORT }
NO. DU PASSEPORT }
A 276159

NAME OF BEARER
NOM DU TITULAIRE }
BACHAN SINGH

ACCOMPANIED BY HIS WIFE
(Maiden name)
ACCOMPAGNE DE SA FEMME
(Née)

{ and by   children }
{ et de   enfants }

NATIONAL STATUS   NATIONALITE

Indian (by birth)

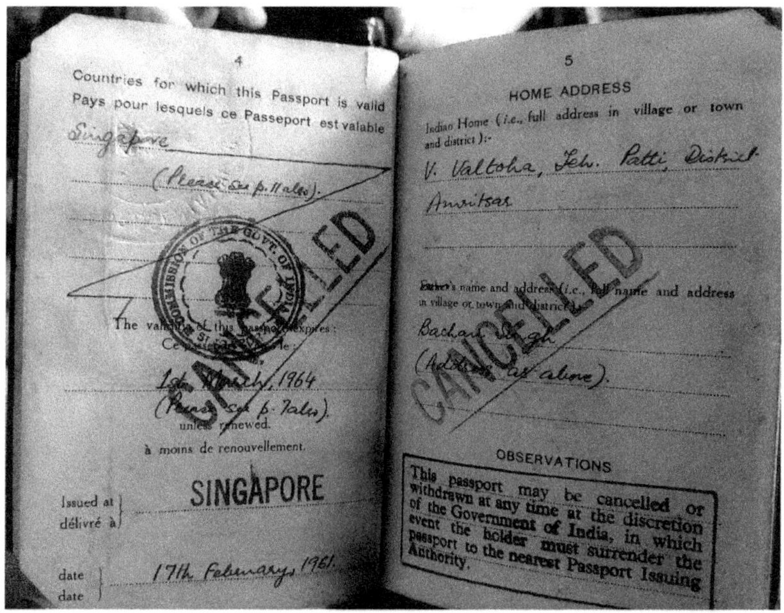

First few pages of Bachan Singh's passport (May 1952). Allegedly, he was born in 1909 but this too may have been falsified for him to be eligible to work in Singapore.

L to R: Teja Singh, Gabriela, Manjit, Nimmi, Kirpal Singh (hidden), me and Kirpal Singh's wife.

The four of us mucking around on a tractor in the fields of the Punjabi countryside. The irony, of my grandfather moving away from this and us paying to return to it, is gold.

ABOUT THE AUTHOR

Hamant Singh is a Singaporean writer who is inspired by the Sublime in horror, different cultures and the occult. *VALTOHA* is his fourth release after *The Sibyl* (2002), *CHAOS: RRR* (2023) and a poetry collaboration called *NÁUSEA | CONFESIÓN* (2023).

After a poem was nominated for the 2022 Rhysling Award by the Science Fiction Poetry Association, *The Sibyl* was listed on the preliminary ballot for the 2023 Bram Stoker Awards (Superior Achievement in a Poetry Collection). In 2023, *The Sibyl* was also nominated for the Elgin Award. Hamant currently resides in Guadalajara, Mexico where he is currently working on an art/poetry collaboration with Irish artist, Shane Reilly and other different projects.